Yannick Grotholt – Writer

Comicon – Artist

PAPERCUTZ™

New York

LEGO CHIMA Graphic Novels Available from PAPERCUTZ™

Coming Soon!

Graphic Novel #1
"High Risk!"

Graphic Novel #2
"The Right Decision"

Graphic Novel #3
"CHI Quest!"

LEGENDS OF CHIMA
#2 "The Right Decision"

Yannick Grotholt – Writer
Comicon – Artist
Tom Orzechowski – Letterer
Max Gartman – Editorial Intern
Beth Scorzato – Production Coordinator
Michael Petranek – Editor
Jim Salicrup
Editor-in-Chief

ISBN: 978-1-62991-074-1 paperback edition
ISBN: 978-1-62991-075-8 hardcover edition

Printed in Canada
August 2014 by Friesens Printing
1 Printer Way
Altona, MB R0G 0B0

Papercutz books may be purchased for business or promotional use. For information on bulk purchases please contact Macmillan Corporate and Premium Sales Department at (800) 221-7945 x5442.

FSC
www.fsc.org
MIX
Paper from
responsible sources
FSC® C016245

LEGO LEGENDS OF CHIMA graphic novels are available for $7.99 in paperback, $12.99 hardcover. Available from booksellers everywhere. You can also order online from Papercutz.com. Or call 1-800-886-1223, Monday through Friday, 9-5 EST. MC, Visa, and AmEx accepted. To order by mail, please add $4.00 for postage and handling for first book ordered, $1.00 for each additional book and make check payable to NBM Publishing. Send to: Papercutz, 160 Broadway, Suite 700, East Wing, New York, NY 10038.

LEGO LEGENDS OF CHIMA graphic novels are also available digitally wherever e-books are sold.

Distributed by Macmillan
First Papercutz Printing

THE RIGHT DECISION

IN A DARING RESCUE MISSION OUR HEROES HAVE FREED THE **RAVEN LEGEND BEAST** FROM THE CLUTCHES OF THE SCORPIONS. THE YOUNG WARRIORS TRAVEL TO CHIMA TO BRING THE GOOD NEWS TO THE RAVEN TRIBE...

ERIS, WHAT'S TROUBLING YOU? AREN'T YOU HAPPY WITH WHAT WE ACHIEVED?

OF COURSE I AM, **LAVAL.** I WAS JUST WONDERING WHAT WILL BECOME OF US ONCE WE HAVE SAVED CHIMA.

I'LL BECOME KING AND YOU'LL BE THE LEADER OF THE EAGLES' COUNCIL, WHAT ELSE?

BUT THE COUNCIL HAS NEVER HAD A SHE-EAGLE AS A MEMBER, NOT TO MENTION AS A LEADER.

EVERYONE, LOOK!

THE EAGLES ARE UNDER ATTACK FROM A SWARM OF BATS! WE MUST HELP THEM.

4

BAM

BAM

HAS ANYONE BEEN INJURED?

WE HAVE THE SITUATION UNDER CONTROL-- FOR NOW. BUT THERE IS ANOTHER PROBLEM...

EQUILA'S ULTRA STRIKER HAD TO MAKE AN EMERGENCY LANDING ON A TREETOP. NOW IT'S ABOUT TO CRASH DOWN ON THE BEAVERS' VILLAGE. TAKE THIS CHI AND HELP THEM!

BUT WOULDN'T IT MAKE MORE SENSE TO USE THE LAST CHI ORBS AGAINST THE BATS?

IN TIMES OF CRISIS WE MUST THINK OF THE GOOD OF CHIMA'S INHABITANTS. THE BEAVERS WOULD OTHERWISE LOSE ALL THEIR HOMES.

COME ON, WE'LL TAKE AN *EAGLE INTERCEPTOR!*

RAZAR, WHAT ABOUT YOU?

BAM

BAM

I'M GOING TO RELIEVE THE BATS OF A FEW TRINKETS.

6

Back in the Outlands, Eris and Laval are planning their attack on the bats...

So, how do we make our *CHI* explode?

But before Laval can respond...

My eagle interceptor! The strangler grass is devouring it!

What the--?!

The *CHI?!*

BLISTA and *BRAPTOR!* They've taken Laval and the *CHI!*

Looking for this?

...and this?

9

ZZZZZZZ

SORRY TO WAKE YOU, MASTER-- YOU HAVE VISITORS.

WHAT ARE YOU WAITING FOR? *SEIZE THEM!*

BUT BEFORE THE BATS CAN REACT, ERIS MAKES A SHOCKING PROPOSAL...

WAIT! I HAVE CAPTURED LAVAL, THE LION WARRIOR. I'LL TRADE HIM FOR FOUR *CHI* ORBS.

WHY SHOULD I ACCEPT YOUR OFFER?

MY FATHER IS KING LAGRAVIS. HE WOULD GIVE HIS ENTIRE KINGDOM IN EXCHANGE FOR ME. AND A KINGDOM IS WORTH MORE THAN FOUR *CHI* ORBS.

THE BATTLE IS STILL RAGING AT EAGLES' SPIRE...

I CAN'T FIRE OFF ANY TORPEDOES WITHOUT HITTING EAGLES AS WELL!

I'LL USE THE TRIPOD CANNON.

LET'S SEE WHAT YOU'VE GOT.

CHOOM

CHOOM

LAVAL'S AIM IS TRUE! THREE BATS LOSE THEIR BALANCE AND PLUNGE INTO THE DEEP...

BULL'S-EYE!

LAVAL! ABOVE US... THE SWARM!

AFTER A STRENUOUS DAY, THE HEROES HAVE PITCHED CAMP IN A DESERT IN THE *OUTLANDS*. THEIR *LEGEND BEASTS* ARE WITH THEM AND GUARD OVER THEM. ALL THE YOUNG WARRIORS HAVE TO DO NOW IS FIND THE WOLF LEGEND BEAST AND THE LION LEGEND BEAST!

A TRUE WOLF

IN THE MIDDLE OF THE NIGHT, *WORRIZ* CREEPS OUT OF THE TENT...

≈ZZZZ≈

≈ZZZZ≈

≈ZZZZ≈

...BUT WORRIZ'S ACTIONS HAVE NOT GONE UNNOTICED BY *LAVAL* AND *CRAGGER*...

THAT'S THE THIRD TIME HE'S SNUCK OUT THIS WEEK.

COME ON, LET'S FOLLOW HIM!

WHERE'S HE GOING AT THIS TIME OF NIGHT?

LET'S FIND OUT!

VROOOOM

YOU'RE NOT THE WOLF LEGEND BEAST! BUT YOUR SCENT IS SOMEHOW FAMILIAR. WHO ARE YOU?

WITHOUT ANSWERING, THE STRANGER ATTACKS!

AT THAT MOMENT, LAVAL AND CRAGGER LEAP OUT TO DEFEND WORRIZ...

WHOA! STEP BACK, HOODED VILLAIN!

FOR A MOMENT, IT SEEMS THE ATTACKER RETREATS...

STOMP

22

PACT WITH THE SPIDER QUEEN

CLANG

THERE HASN'T BEEN ANOTHER ATTACK BY THE SPIDERS FOR DAYS NOW, CRAGGER! SOMETHING'S IN THE WIND.

AGREED, LAVAL! WE'VE GOT TO KEEP TRAINING HARD TO STAY FIT!

IN THE MEANTIME, THE OTHER HEROES HAVE DECIDED TO RETURN TO CHIMA FOR A DAY TO VISIT THEIR TRIBES.

DON'T FORGET YOUR CUPCAKES! YOU'RE WELCOME TO SHARE THEM WITH YOUR TRIBES, BUT FOR GOODNESS' SAKE DON'T LET ON WHO BAKED THEM!

IT'S NOT A GOOD IDEA TO LEAVE THE OUTLANDS. THE SPIDERS ARE UP TO SOMETHING-- I CAN FEEL IT!

BESIDES, WE STILL HAVE TO FIND MY FATHER AND *LAVAL'S LION LEGEND BEAST!*

WE'LL ONLY BE GONE FOR A DAY. THE LAST FEW WEEKS HAVE BEEN REALLY TOUGH-- YOU SHOULD TAKE A BREAK!

A BREAK IS OUT OF THE QUESTION-- WE'RE SWORN TO PROTECT CHIMA FROM ANY KIND OF DANGER, NO MATTER HOW SMALL!

WE'LL HOLD THE FORT HERE. GIVE MY REGARDS TO MY FATHER.

OKAY! SO LONG!

CRAGGER, PACK YOUR THINGS. WE'RE TAKING A TRIP.

WHERE TO?

"SPIDER CANYON!"

CAREFUL--THIS IS SPIDER COUNTRY. OUR ENEMIES COULD BE HIDING ANYWHERE.

THAT'S NOT WHAT I CALL HIDING.

THE SPIDERS CERTAINLY ARE UP TO SOMETHING. SPIDER QUEEN **SPINLYN** WANTS TO ATTACK THE LION TEMPLE AND IS RECRUITING SPIDER SOLDIERS FROM ALL OVER THE OUTLANDS...

SPIDERS FROM THE NORTH, EAST, SOUTH, AND WEST! I AM DELIGHTED THAT YOU HAVE TAKEN THE LONG JOURNEY TO SPIDER CANYON UPON YOURSELVES!

I HAVE RECRUITED YOU FROM ALL OVER THE OUTLANDS FOR ONE PURPOSE--TO ATTACK THE LION TEMPLE! THIS VERY DAY WE WILL *OVERTHROW KING LAGRAVIS* AND *SEIZE CHIMA!*

MEANWHILE IN THE SWAMP: KING LAGRAVIS HAS ORDERED A SQUAD OF CROCODILE SOLDIERS FROM QUEEN CRUNKET-- AROUSING SUSPICION IN CROOLER, CRAGGER'S TWIN SISTER.

I DON'T WANT TO HEAR ANY MORE OF THAT, CROOLER. YOU HAVE ALREADY DONE ENOUGH DAMAGE OVER THE LAST FEW MONTHS. GO TO YOUR ROOM AND THINK ABOUT THE ERROR OF YOUR WAYS.

THE LIONS ARE SUPPOSED TO BE FOLLOWING OUR ORDERS, NOT THE OTHER WAY AROUND. AS SOON AS CHIMA IS FREED THEY'LL STAB US IN THE BACK. LET'S BEAT THEM TO IT AND MAKE RUGS OUT OF THEM.

LATER, CRAGGER AND LAVAL ARRIVE AT THE CROCODILE TEMPLE...

MY SON! DID YOU FIND YOUR FATHER AND FREE THE LION LEGEND BEAST?

I'M AFRAID NOT. WE FEAR SPINLYN PLANS TO ROB OUR ARMORY. SHE HAS CALLED SPIDER SOLDIERS FROM ALL OVER AND PLANS TO ATTACK THE LION TEMPLE.

THIS IS TROUBLE-SOME. WE MUST SEND TWICE AS MANY SOLDIERS TO KING LAGRAVIS.

CRUG, PUT MORE SOLDIERS ON THE CROC BOAT. BUT KEEP TWO PLACES FREE. CRAGGER AND LAVAL ARE ALSO TRAVELING TO THE LION TEMPLE.

AS YOU WISH, QUEEN CRUNKET.

KA-CHING

36

40

BUT CROOLER STILL HAS AN ACE UP HER SLEEVE...

OH, NO YOU DON'T. ORDER YOUR SOLDIERS TO GO BACK WHERE THEY CAME FROM. BUT FIRST, TAKE YOUR WEAPONS BACK TO THE CROCODILE'S ARMORY.

THE SCENT OF THE **PERSUADER PLANT** BEFUDDLES SPINLYN'S SENSES, FORCING HER TO FULFILL CROOLER'S DEMANDS...

LISTEN, MY FRIENDS. THERE IS NOTHING FOR US HERE. CHIMA IS EVEN MORE DESOLATE THAN THE OUTLANDS. LET US GO HOME.

NOW THAT WE'RE BACK IN CHIMA WE SHOULD TAKE A TIME-OUT. WHAT DO YOU THINK?

EXCUSE ME...

SO YOU'VE CHANGED YOUR MIND ABOUT THE LIONS?

DREAM ON! I WILL NEVER CHANGE MY MIND ABOUT THE LIONS!

EXCUSE ME, LAVAL, BUT MY SISTER AND I HAVE *FAMILY BUSINESS* TO DISCUSS!

GOOD LUCK, MY FRIEND!

CRAGGER KNOWS HIS SISTER IS NO LONGER AS BAD AS SHE USED TO BE. ONE DAY THEY WILL GET ALONG BETTER AND FIGHT SIDE BY SIDE TO PROTECT CHIMA FROM A MAJOR DISASTER...

the end

44

45

50

THE SPIDERS AND BATS HAVE BEEN DEFEATED. LAVAL AND HIS FRIENDS RETURN TO A HERO'S WELCOME.

I'VE NEVER SEEN SUCH A BIG CELEBRATION!

KING LAGRAVIS BEGINS...

YOU SHALL EACH BE REWARDED FOR YOUR HEROIC DEEDS...

...WITHOUT YOU, CHIMA WOULD HAVE BEEN LOST FOREVER. WE ARE ETERNALLY GRATEFUL.

BUT PEACE IS NOT FOR LONG IN CHIMA...

FOR A NEW THREAT IS ON THE HORIZON... ONE GREATER THAN LAVAL AND HIS FRIENDS HAVE EVER SEEN.

TO BE CONTINUED!

WATCH OUT FOR PAPERCUTZ™

Welcome to the sensational second LEGO® LEGENDS OF CHIMA graphic novel, by Yannick Grotholt and Comicon, from Papercutz, those Chi-powered people dedicated to publishing great graphic novels for all ages. I'm Jim Salicrup, the Editor-in-Chief and Crooler's on-call beauty consultant. I'm here to offer up news, behind-the-scenes info, and sincere thanks. Let's start with the thanking...

My partner, Papercutz publisher Terry Nantier, and the entire hard-working staff of Papercutz and I want to express how grateful we are to you for your support of the LEGO LEGENDS OF CHIMA graphic novel series. Papercutz is just a teeny-tiny company, trying its very best to provide you with the kind of entertaining comics that you love, competing against countless competitors, many of them huge media corporations! And thanks to the wonderful folks at LEGO, we are fortunate enough to bring you the characters you love in all-new comics form. As a result, our very first LEGO LEGENDS OF CHIMA graphic novel was a big success—for which we thank you!

If this is actually your very first LEGO LEGENDS OF CHIMA graphic novel, we thank you for your support too! And don't worry—the collectors' item first graphic novel is still available at bookstores, comicbook stores, online booksellers, and us (see page 2). Just as most of the LEGO Group fans love collecting LEGO sets of their favorite characters, we know LEGO fans want to collect our graphic novels as well. Believe us—we know! We've had to break the news to frustrated LEGO fans more than once that certain hardcover editions of LEGO BIONICLE graphic novels are currently sold out.

As for news, be sure to mark your calendars—coming to a theater near you on September 23, 2016 is the all-new LEGO NINJAGO 3D movie! Yeah, we know—that seems so far away! But in the meantime, one of the most exciting events in the world of LEGO happens in the 10th LEGO NINJAGO graphic novel-- available right now! It's the dramatic debut of the Phantom Ninja! The only place you can find this exciting new Ninjago character is exclusively in the pages of NINJAGO #10 "The Phantom Ninja"! We're already getting bombarded at Papercutz with countless requests to create an all-new Phantom Ninja graphic novel series—fans are that excited about this new character! See for yourself what all the fuss is about—before the graphic novel sells out!

Finally, a little behind-the-scenes info. Many of you have wondered who this mysterious "Comicon," that was listed in the art credits in the premiere LEGO LEGENDS OF CHIMA graphic novel, might be. The answer is that it's the name of the comic art studio providing the stunning visuals for the actual comic art pages! Specifically, for LEGO LEGENDS OF CHIMA #1, it was: Miguel Sanchez, pencil art; Marc Alberich, ink art; and Oriol San Julian, color art. Together they are "Comicon" and they did a beautiful job illustrating Yannick Grotholt's scripts!

Speaking of which, don't miss Grotholt and Comicon's next collaboration in LEGO THE LEGENDS OF CHIMA #3 "CHI Quest!" coming soon!

Long Live Laval!

Thanks,

JiM

STAY IN TOUCH!

EMAIL: salicrup@papercutz.com
WEB: papercutz.com
TWITTER: @papercutzgn
FACEBOOK: PAPERCUTZGRAPHICNOVELS
FAN MAIL: Papercutz, ¹60 Broadway, Suite 700, East Wing, New York, NY 10038

KIDS GO FREE

with full price adult ticket to LEGOLAND® Parks or LEGOLAND Discovery Centers
Purchase this offer at **LEGOLAND.com/LEGOPapercutz** now through 12/31/2015.

Offer good for one free one-day child ticket with purchase of a full-price one-day adult ticket to LEGOLAND® California, LEGOLAND Florida or LEGOLAND Discovery Centers. Valid for one complimentary child. Offer cannot be applied to pre-purchased, two day tickets, memberships, online ticket sales or combined with any other discounts or offers. No photocopies or facsimiles will be accepted. Additional restrictions may apply. Prices and hours subject to change without notice. The right of final interpretation resides with LEGOLAND. Not for resale. **Expires 12/31/2015.**
Discount ID 149930

LEGO, the LEGO logo, the Brick and Knob configurations, the Minifigure and LEGOLAND are trademarks of the LEGO Group.
©2014 The LEGO Group. LEGOLAND IS A PART OF THE MERLIN ENTERTAINMENTS GROUP.

Atlanta • Boston • Chicago • Dallas/Fort Worth
Kansas City • Toronto • Westchester

Indoor Attraction • LEGO Rides • LEGO MINILAND • 4D Cinema • LEGO Factory Tour • Play Zone • Birthday Room • Shop & Cafe